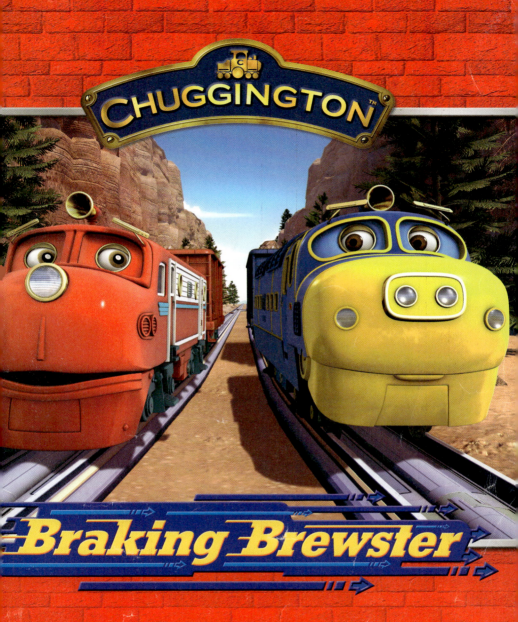

CHUGGINGTON™

Braking Brewster

Adapted by Mara Conlon
Based on the story by Sarah Ball and Kate Fawkes

SCHOLASTIC INC.
New York Toronto London Auckland
Sydney Mexico City New Delhi Hong Kong

ISBN 978-0-545-26632-1

© Ludorum plc 2011. Chuggington™ is a trademark of Ludorum plc. All rights reserved. Published by Scholastic Inc. SCHOLASTIC and associated logos are trademarks and/or registered trademarks of Scholastic Inc.

12 11 10 9 8 7 6 5 4 3 2 1   11 12 13 14 15 16/0

Printed in the U.S.A.   40
First printing, April 2011

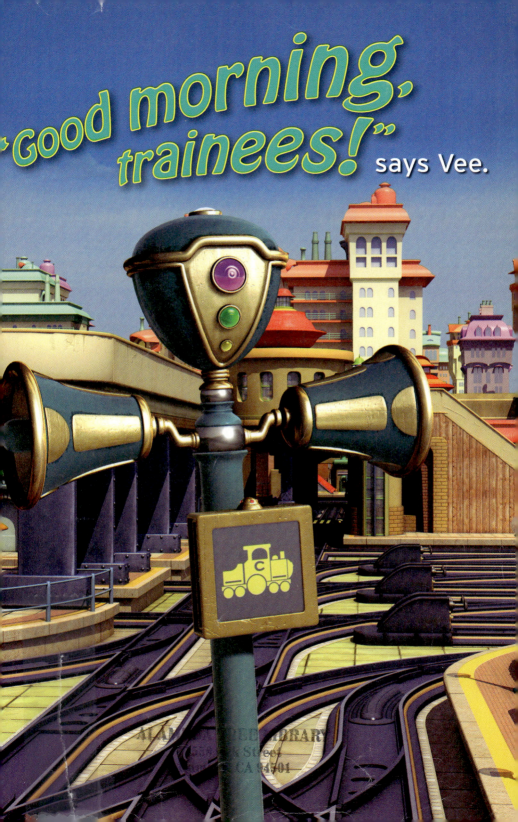

"Good morning, trainees!" says Vee.

"Brewster and Wilson, please report to the training yard. Dunbar has a job for you."

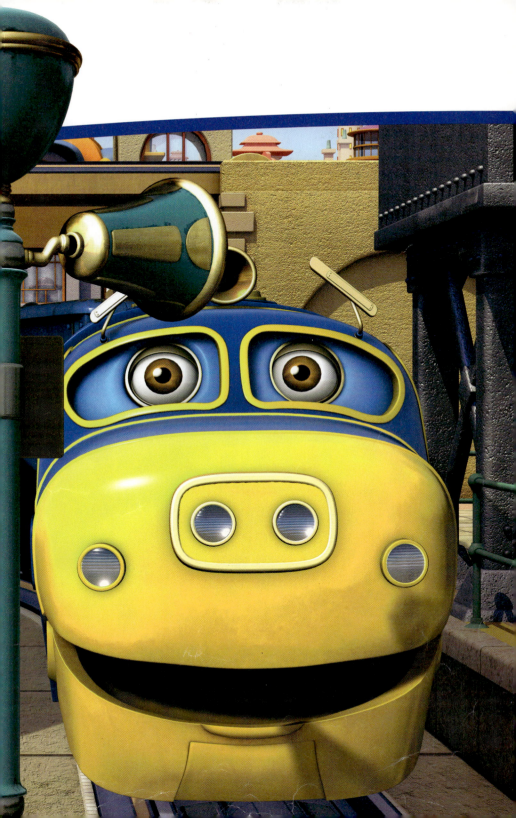

First Dunbar shows them
how to use a hopper car.

The hopper car has a door in the bottom. It can open and close.

"Your job is to take the cars to the top of the mountain," says Dunbar.

"Pick up some rocks and bring them to the yard."

"Going downhill is harder with a big load," says Dunbar.

Brewster and Wilson go up, up, up.

Brewster closes the door of his hopper car. He fills his car with rocks.

"I am strong," he says.

Brewster takes all the rocks.
"There is only dust left for me
to carry," says Wilson sadly.

"Sorry!" says Brewster.
The trainees start their trip back
to the yard.

"Come on, slowpoke!"

shouts Brewster.

"Slow down!" shouts Wilson.

"Dunbar told us to go slowly!"

But it is too late.
The load is too big.
Brewster's brakes do not work!
He loses control.

"Honking horns! I'm going too fast!"
Brewster shouts.

"**Help!**" he cries.

Wilson pulls ahead of Brewster.
He opens his hopper car door.
The dust falls on the tracks.

The brakes can grip the dust.
Now Brewster can stop!

"You saved me!"

says Brewster.

"That is what friends are for!"
says Wilson.

Wilson and Brewster finish the job.
"Good work, chuggers!" says Vee.

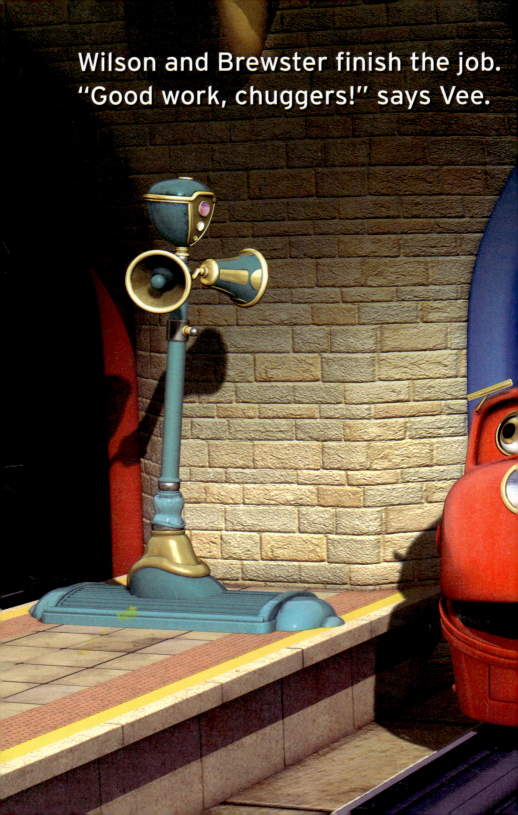

Then, the trainees go to tell Dunbar their story.

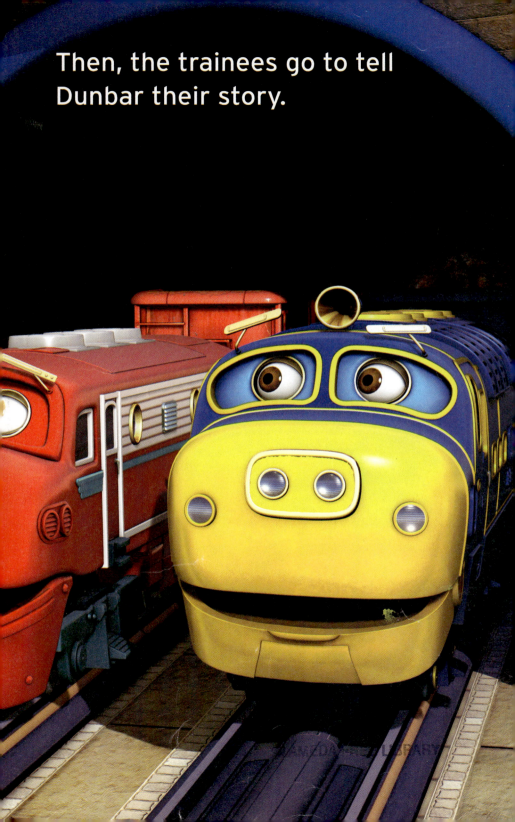

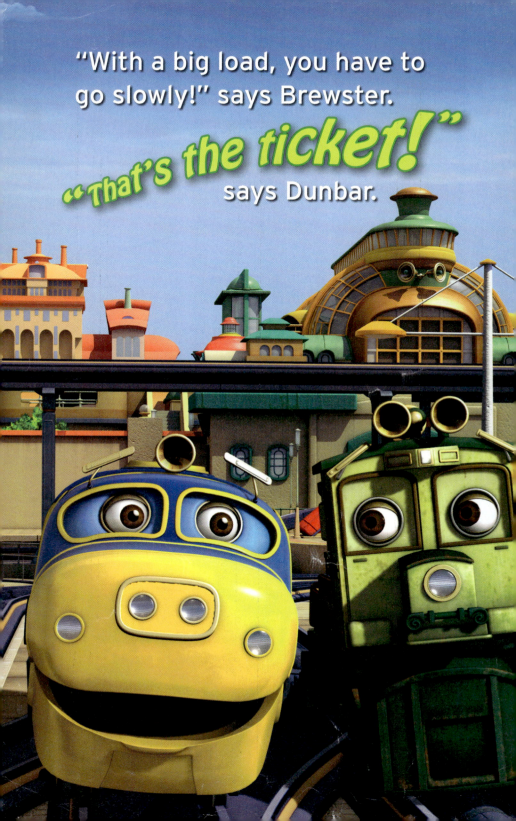

"With a big load, you have to go slowly!" says Brewster.

"That's the ticket!" says Dunbar.